Taking Arthritis to School

by DeeDee L. Miller

Adapted for the Special Kids in School® series
created by Kim Gosselin

JayJo Books

Publishing Special Books for Special Kids®

Published by
JayJo Books
A Brand of The Guidance Group
Publishing Special Books for Special Kids®

JayJo Books is a publisher of books to help teachers, parents, and children cope with chronic illnesses, special needs, and health education in classroom, family, and social settings.

Library of Congress Control Number: 2002108360
ISBN 10: 1-891383-21-3
ISBN 13: 978-1-891383-21-2

First Edition
Thirteenth book in our *Special Kids in School*® series

For information about
Premium and Special Sales, contact:
JayJo Books
The Guidance Group
www.guidance-group.com

The opinions in this book are solely those of the author. Medical care is highly individualized and should never be altered without professional medical consultation.

Dedication

This book is dedicated to my son Eric Raymond Robert Miller,
a senior at Syracuse University, Syracuse, NY and to all children living with
the many forms of arthritis.

A Note from the Author

Eric has always been an inspiration to all who meet him. No matter what pain or surgery he endured, he always smiled and said he was fine. Eric does not let arthritis get in his way. Many nights when his joints were throbbing, I would pray he would receive a restful sleep. I thank God for giving us peace and hope.

As a third grade teacher, I believe literature is powerful. It is my hope that Taking Arthritis to School will educate kids, parents, friends, families, and classmates regarding the unique needs of children living with arthritis.

My entire family wins applause for their support and love during the years Eric had juvenile rheumatoid arthritis. The majority of his pain is now gone. He is majoring in Industrial Design and is the coxswain on the Men's Varsity Crew Team in college! Cheers also to Kathleen Powers at The Central New York Arthritis Foundation for her encouragement and assistance.

DeeDee Miller

Hi! My name is Eric. I live in a blue house with my mom, my dad, my brother Jason, and our dog, Butch. I love riding my bike, and I'm a Cub Scout. I love making things and taking things apart. And, I have arthritis. Arthritis is a disease you can't see. It makes my joints get hot, swollen, and painful. Joints are where bones connect.

Arthritis is only ONE part of me. In other ways, I'm just a kid like you!

I wasn't born with arthritis. When I was seven, I had a high fever and a rash. My legs and wrists hurt. Something else was weird...I couldn't walk right! My mom took me to the doctor's office. To cheer me up, she drew a clown on one of those sticks the doctor uses to make you say, "Aahh."

I could tell my doctor was concerned. He kept watching me while I tried walking back and forth in his office.

I visited a rheumatologist (roo-mah-tol-o-jist) for more tests. A rheumatologist is a doctor who helps people with arthritis. The nurse took blood from a vein in my arm for a blood test. It only hurt for a second. I liked to watch while the doctor moved my wrists, arms, knees, ankles, and hips to check for stiffness or swelling.

The rheumatologist told my mom and dad I had Juvenile Rheumatoid Arthritis (JRA). Every month, I would need blood tests. I would need X-rays and special pictures of my bones, called bone scans, to see how I was growing. Twice a year, my eyes would have to be checked. JRA can show up in lots of different places in your body...even in your eyes or your neck.

Mom and Dad were surprised. They didn't even know kids could get arthritis!

My dad put up an extra railing on our stairs, so I could hold on to both sides. He put a big handle in the bathtub to help me pull myself out.

I spend a lot of time soaking in my bathtub. While I soak, I do science experiments with colored water, paint pictures, and try to see how high I can make the bubbles rise.

Soaking can be fun, and it helps me feel better!

I also do exercises in warm water, with other kids with arthritis. LuAnn, my physical (fis-a-cul) therapist, helps exercise my joints, while we play games with balls and sticks. She teaches us swimming strokes. My favorite is the butterfly. I feel like a fish flying through the water.

I don't hurt at all in the water. Swimming is so much fun!

My mom rubs special creams on my joints and gives me medicine the doctor prescribes. I use wraps heated in the microwave to help my joints feel better. Instead of hot wraps, some kids with arthritis use a cold pack of ice or even a bag of frozen veggies, like peas. At school, my friends help me by carrying my books and lunch tray.

I do whatever it takes to get to school. Even if I have to limp or walk slowly, I don't want to miss going to school and seeing my friends!

Sometimes kids with arthritis have unexpected problems. Last year, my right hip was inflamed, and I had to go to the hospital to have surgery. I was in a cast for seven weeks. I used a wheelchair and then neat red metal crutches I picked out myself. My nurse, Sue, gave me ice cream and a stuffed gorilla. I had lessons at home from my teacher. My friends thought I was the luckiest kid.

But, all I wanted to do was go to school. I hate to miss anything!

I had a great idea for my science project. I drew a poster and wrote a report about arthritis. I showed the other kids the exercises that help my joints move. My science project helped them understand why I can't always run and why I sometimes need piggyback rides.

The kids learned that arthritis isn't contagious. They can't catch it from me, and it's okay for them to play with me and be my friends.

Having arthritis feels different every day. Some days, I wake up ready to run. Other days, it's hard getting out of my bed. Mom or Dad may have to carry me to the bathtub, so I can soak in hot water.

On days like that, I have to stay home and rest. Then, I like to play video games with my brother. My friend Louie and I made up a band called Ice Cream and Candy, and we like to sing together. My cousin Pat and I pretend we are professional wrestlers. Once, we made up a magazine about wrestling, and we even drew pictures for it.

Keeping busy helps me feel better!

My hands and wrists puff up and ache sometimes. When they do, it's hard for me to hold my fork or my pencil, or to open doors. It's easier for me to hold onto things with fatter handles. That way, my hand doesn't cramp up as much.

When my pain goes away for a long time, I am in remission (ree-mish-un). I like that time best of all!

Resting, eating well, and exercising help me live better with arthritis. When my joints swell and hurt, I have another neat way to help myself...I think of ways that will make them feel better. One of my ideas is to design a pair of heated sneakers with a blow-up cushion. When I grow up, I want to design things to help kids with arthritis.

I may have arthritis, but it doesn't have me!

LET'S TAKE THE ARTHRITIS KIDS' QUIZ!

1. What is arthritis?

Arthritis is a disease that makes my joints hurt and feel hot and swollen. Joints are where bones connect with each other. Sometimes arthritis gets better or worse, but it doesn't go away.

2. Do kids get arthritis in all their joints?

Every kid with arthritis is affected differently. My wrists, knees, hips, ankles, and hands all have arthritis. Some days, all my joints bother me. Other days, just one or two hurt.

3. Can you see arthritis?

Arthritis is in my joints, and you can't see it. When my joints hurt, you may see me limp or walk slowly. My fingers and hands may be swollen and they may curl in a bit.

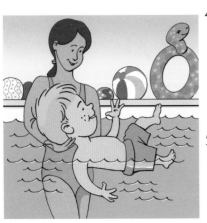

4. What does a rheumatologist do?

A rheumatologist is a doctor who helps people with arthritis. My doctor gave me exercises to help me move better and medicine to help with the swelling that causes me pain.

5. What does a physical therapist do?

A physical therapist helps you exercise different parts of your body that hurt or can't move well. I have a physical therapist at my swim group, and I had another to help me walk when my casts came off.

6. How can you play with a friend who lives with arthritis?

That's easy! Your friend may not always be able to run or jump. If your friend is in pain, you can do something less active, like playing a board game, drawing, using a computer, or enjoying music together.

7. At school, what can you do for a friend with arthritis?

Walk alongside your friend. At times, he may need to walk slowly. Help him by carrying his books or lunch tray and by opening doors. Sometimes, he may feel fine and want to do things himself, so it's a good idea to ask first before helping.

8. What can you do when you are in pain?

I can take a hot bath or shower, rub special creams on my joints, lay a hot or cold pack on my joints, and rest or nap. I can take my medications, breathe deeply, and relax while listening to music or watching a movie.

9. Can you play sports with arthritis?

Sure! What makes me feel best is SWIMMING. Swimming and bike riding are the best exercises to move my joints correctly.

10. How does having arthritis make you feel?

When I can't do what the other kids do, I sometimes feel sad. But, I've learned how to live with arthritis. When I get real sad, I talk it out with my family. They always come up with new ideas to try!

Great job! Thanks for taking the Arthritis Kids' Quiz!

Ten Tips For Teachers

 1. GET TO KNOW YOUR STUDENT.
Find out what activities your student living with arthritis enjoys. Build on those interests by encouraging participation in new areas in art, music, drama, creative writing, and nonphysical activities. Check with the child's last teacher for helpful tips; at the end of the school year, share those tips with his next teacher.

 2. BE AN ADVOCATE FOR YOUR STUDENT.
Establish a relationship that enables the child to be comfortable telling you how he feels. Watch for signs that the child is in physical pain, or feeling sad or left out. If necessary, refer the student to the school nurse, social worker, etc. If the child needs help, assist him in a way that doesn't make him stand out as being different. Instead, encourage discussion about the ways all students are alike.

 3. LISTEN TO THE STUDENT WITH ARTHRITIS.
When her joints are stiff or she has been sitting too long, the child with arthritis may need to get up and move. Allow her to pass out papers, water plants, or do errands to stretch her painful joints. Believe your student if she says she needs to lie down and rest. Swollen joints do need rest, and it's difficult to concentrate when joints are inflamed. Have a permanent pass on hand to save you time and the child embarrassment when she needs to visit the nurse. Create a secret signal so the student can slip out quietly.

 4. BE SENSITIVE TO DELIVERY OF DRUG PROGRAMS.
Students taking prescribed medicines may be concerned by discussion about the negative aspects of taking drugs. Help your students understand the difference between prescribed and street drugs and the importance of following their doctor's instructions.

5. INCLUDE THE STUDENT WITH ARTHRITIS IN ALL ACTIVITIES.
Let your student decide how she is feeling and what her activity level should be on any given day. If your student is reluctant to participate or experiences pain during a game, modify the

game so the child is still involved. Ideas include: running the stopwatch, pairing with a buddy, keeping score, or being the announcer. Choose games that promote fairness and teamwork and are not physically competitive.

 6. ALLOW MODIFICATIONS.
Request materials and equipment to assist the student who lives with arthritis, such as a tape recorder, a voice-activated laptop computer, and wider pencils/markers with grips. Allow another student to scribe during writing assignments when necessary. Issue an extra set of textbooks for home usage.

 7. MAP OUT THE SHORTEST ROUTES.
Students with arthritis may walk more slowly than other children and may limp at times. Plan out the shortest routes in school and for field trips that involve walking. Have an elevator key to use if necessary. Do not assume the child will need extra help. Some days he will feel great!

 8. EDUCATE YOUR STUDENTS ABOUT ARTHRITIS.
When students are educated with the facts, they act more responsibly. If your student who lives with arthritis agrees, invite her doctor, physical therapist, parents, and the school nurse into the classroom to talk about arthritis. Use arthritis as the basis for a lesson on Internet research.

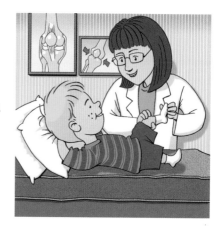

 9. PROMOTE COMMUNICATION WITH THE CHILD'S FAMILY.
Ask parents/guardians about their child's strengths, fears, medications, and hobbies. Welcome their ideas! Ask questions and assure the family that their child can be successful. After an initial conference, have ongoing discussions throughout the year.

 10. LEARN ABOUT ARTHRITIS.
There are 300,000 children living with arthritis and over 100 diseases that involve some form of arthritis. Your local Arthritis Foundation can be a great source of helpful brochures and information.

ADDITIONAL RESOURCES

Kids Get Arthritis Too! (a wellness letter)
P.O. Box 921907
Norcross, GA 30010-1907
1-800-268-6942

Arthritis Foundation
1330 West Peachtree Street
Atlanta, GA 30309
1-800-283-7800
www.arthritis.org

**The American Juvenile Arthritis
Organization (AJAO)**
1330 West Peachtree Street
Atlanta, GA 30309
404-872-7100

American Pain Society
4700 W. Lake Avenue
Glenview, IL 60025
847-375-4715
www.ampainsoc.org

**National Institute of Arthritis
and Musculoskeletal and Skin Diseases
(NIAMS)**
Information Clearinghouse
National Institutes of Health
1 AMS Circle
Bethesda, MD 20892-3675
301-495-4484
www.niams.nih.gov

To order additional copies of *Taking Arthritis to School* or inquire about our quantity discounts for schools, hospitals, and affiliated organizations, contact us at 1-800-999-6884.

From our *Special Kids in School*® series

Taking A.D.D. to School
Taking Asthma to School
Taking Autism to School
Taking Cancer to School
Taking Cerebral Palsy to School
Taking Cystic Fibrosis to School
Taking Depression to School
Taking Diabetes to School
Taking Down Syndrome to School
Taking Dyslexia to School
Taking Food Allergies to School
Taking Seizure Disorders to School
Taking Tourette Syndrome to School
...and others coming soon!

From our new *Healthy Habits for Kids*® series

There's a Louse in My House
A Fun Story about Kids and Head Lice

From our new *Special Family and Friends*™ series

Allie Learns About Alzheimer's Disease
A Family Story about Love, Patience, and Acceptance
Patrick Learns About Parkinson's Disease
A Story of a Special Bond Between Friends
... and others coming soon!

And from our *Substance Free Kids*® series

Smoking STINKS!!™
A Heartwarming Story about the Importance of Avoiding Tobacco

Other books available now!

SPORTSercise!
A School Story about
Exercise-Induced Asthma
ZooAllergy
A Fun Story about Allergy
and Asthma Triggers
Rufus Comes Home
Rufus the Bear with Diabetes™
A Story about Diagnosis and Acceptance
The ABC's of Asthma
An Asthma Alphabet Book
for Kids of All Ages
Taming the Diabetes Dragon
A Story about Living Better
with Diabetes
Trick-or-Treat for Diabetes
A Halloween Story for Kids
Living with Diabetes